# Bossy Wi...

"Hey, Jessica!" Winston shouted. "Why aren't you with the other Indians?" They were just about to begin rehearsal for the school Thanksgiving play.

"Hey, Jessica! Why aren't you with the other Indians?" Jessica repeated, mimicking Winston's bossy voice. "I'm the best actor in the whole world," she said. "I'm going to be a Hollywood star and be in the movies."

"Cut it out, Jessica," Winston said. His face was bright red.

"What's wrong, Win?" Jessica asked. "Are you mad because people are listening to me instead of you?"

Winston looked angry. "Jessica!" he shouted. "You're ruining the rehearsal." He turned around and stomped away.

Bantam Skylark Books in the
SWEET VALLEY KIDS series
Ask your bookseller for the
books you have missed

SWEET VALLEY KIDS

# STARRING WINSTON EGBERT

Written by
Molly Mia Stewart

Created by
FRANCINE PASCAL

Illustrated by
Ying-Hwa Hu

A BANTAM SKYLARK BOOK®
NEW YORK • TORONTO • LONDON • SYDNEY • AUCKLAND

*To Nicole Pascal Johansson*

RL 2, 005–008

STARRING WINSTON EGBERT

*A Bantam Skylark Book / November 1990*

*Sweet Valley High® and Sweet Valley Kids are trademarks of
Francine Pascal*

*Conceived by Francine Pascal*

*Produced by Daniel Weiss Associates, Inc.
33 West 17th Street
New York, NY 10011*

*Cover art by Susan Tang*

ISBN 0-553-15836-8

*Published simultaneously in the United States and Canada*

PRINTED IN THE UNITED STATES OF AMERICA

CWO      0 9 8 7 6 5 4 3 2 1

# CHAPTER 1

## Jessica's New Rival

Elizabeth Wakefield and her twin sister, Jessica, held hands and watched as Lila and Ellen turned the jump rope around.

"One," Elizabeth whispered. "Two," Jessica said. "Three!" they shouted together. The two girls jumped in and started skipping in perfect unison.

Jessica and Elizabeth did a lot of things together. That wasn't surprising because they were identical twins. They looked exactly alike. Both girls had long blond hair with bangs and the same shade of blue-green eyes. When they wore identical outfits, the only way to tell them apart was by looking at their name bracelets. They often told their friends they were just like two peas in a pod.

Just because they looked alike on the outside didn't mean they were the same on the inside. Elizabeth liked reading books and making up adventures to play outside. She was good at school, too, because she tried hard.

Jessica didn't like schoolwork. Instead, she passed notes in class. She preferred to play games that didn't mess up her clothing. And she knew she could always count on Elizabeth to help her with her homework. Even though each had different likes and dislikes, they were still best friends.

"Who wants to switch with me?" Lila Fowler asked. Lila was in the twins' second

grade class at Sweet Valley Elementary School, and she was Jessica's best friend after Elizabeth. "I'm bored turning the rope."

"I'll switch with you," Elizabeth said. She jumped out and looked around the park. Every Sunday afternoon most of their classmates rode their bikes to the park to play on the swings, the seesaw, or the jungle gym. Elizabeth saw Eva Simpson and Amy Sutton arriving and waved to them.

Amy waved back. "Hello," Eva shouted. She had a pretty accent because she had grown up in Jamaica, an island in the West Indies. She had only moved to Sweet Valley recently, but she already had many friends. Amy and Elizabeth were her best friends.

"Do you want a turn?" Elizabeth asked, as Eva and Amy hopped off their bicycles.

"No thanks," Amy answered.

4

"I'll watch," Eva said. "Here come Winston and Todd. I wonder what they want?"

"Not them," Jessica groaned. "Winston is such a show-off."

Elizabeth grinned. Winston Egbert was the class clown.

"Can I have a turn, can I have a turn?" Winston said in a high voice. He danced on his tiptoes and pretended he was one of the girls jumping rope. "It's my favorite thing to do in the whole world!"

Everyone laughed. "Very funny," Lila said, shaking her head. "Don't let him have a turn," she told Elizabeth, who was now holding one end of the rope, and Ellen Riteman, who was holding the other end.

Winston pushed out his lower lip and made his ears stick out, too, which made him look very silly.

"Maybe you'll get a jump rope for Christmas," Todd said, punching Winston in the arm.

"It's not even Thanksgiving yet!" Winston said.

Eva looked at Elizabeth. "What is Thanksgiving? We didn't have that holiday in Jamaica."

"You don't know what Thanksgiving is?" Lila asked.

"It's a holiday about the Pilgrims," Jessica said.

"And the Indians," Todd added.

Eva still looked puzzled, so Elizabeth tried to explain. "When the Pilgrims first came to America," she began, "they nearly starved during their first winter. The Indians helped them and brought them food. Then they all had a big feast together—"

"And the Pilgrims gave thanks that they survived," Amy cut in.

"They were thankful they didn't die of starvation," Winston added. He grabbed his stomach and made a horrible face.

Elizabeth nodded. "Or from the freezing cold. So every year we have a big dinner to say thank you."

"That's how the holiday got its name. Give thanks. Thanksgiving," she said slowly.

"I get it," Eva said with a smile. "Thanksgiving sounds like a good holiday. It sounds as nice as our Independence Day we had in Jamaica."

"And," Lila added in her know-it-all way, "there's always a Thanksgiving play at school."

Elizabeth saw the excited look on her sister's face. Their teacher had already told

7

them that this year the first, second, and third graders would be putting on the Thanksgiving play. Every year different grades were chosen. Jessica had been hoping to get a big part. She liked to be the center of attention.

"And I'll be the star," Winston announced.

Jessica frowned. "You will not," she said. "You're too goofy to be in the play."

"Says who?" Winston asked.

Jessica turned her back on him. Winston started making funny faces at her even though she couldn't see. The others laughed.

"Maybe you'll both get parts," Elizabeth pointed out.

Jessica folded her arms and lifted her chin in the air. "I wouldn't want to be in a play with Winston. He would just ruin it."

Winston folded his arms and lifted his chin

in the air, too. "Then I guess you won't be in the play," he teased.

"Oh, brother," Lila said. She wondered what Jessica would really do if they both got parts.

# CHAPTER 2

# Pilgrim Life

During social studies on Monday, Mrs. Otis showed slides of the Pilgrims' village.

"This is the way Plymouth Plantation looked almost four hundred years ago," she explained. "The houses fell down, but some historians rebuilt them to look just like the originals."

Elizabeth stared at the tiny log cabins. A man was standing next to one of them, and he was almost as tall as the whole house.

"They had to live in those?" Ken Matthews asked. "They look like play houses."

"Here's a picture of the inside," Mrs. Otis went on. A slide of a dark room with a fireplace and a dirt floor clicked into the projector. "Everyone in the family lived in one room."

"I could never live there," Lila proclaimed. "I'd have to have my own room."

"You're spoiled," Charlie Cashman muttered. Everyone knew that Lila's parents gave her whatever she wanted.

"They had to do all their cooking in a small fireplace like this," Mrs. Otis continued.

Elizabeth looked at her sister. She knew they were thinking the same thing: It looked like fun but their warm and cozy house was a lot nicer!

"Many of the Pilgrims died during their first winter in Massachusetts," the teacher explained. "The weather was a lot colder than what they were used to in England, and they were not prepared. They were cold and hungry and sick all the time."

Caroline Pearce raised her hand. "Why didn't they go back to where they came from?"

"They couldn't," Mrs. Otis said. "They had left England planning never to return. Besides, in those days you couldn't travel in the winter, especially by ship."

Elizabeth shivered. She tried to imagine her fingers and toes going numb. "It must have been hard to be a Pilgrim," she said.

Mrs. Otis nodded. "It certainly was."

"But the Indians rescued them, right?"

Elizabeth went on. "I'll bet it was exciting to meet the Indians."

"That's right," Todd said. "They knew how to hunt and fish, and they had warm clothing for the winter."

The other boys agreed. "The Indians were great," Winston said.

"Mrs. Otis!" Jessica raised her hand and waved it. "Mrs. Otis?"

The teacher turned off the projector now that all the slides had been shown. "Yes?" she asked while she turned on the lights.

"Will there be an Indian princess part in the Thanksgiving play?" Jessica asked in an excited voice.

"No, I'm sorry, Jessica," Mrs. Otis said. "There isn't a part for an Indian princess in this play."

Jessica frowned. "But will there be a beautiful Indian girl part with lots of lines to say?"

"There will be several parts for Indian boys and girls," Mrs. Otis said. She smiled. "But I'm not going to give away all the secrets. The tryouts for the play are tomorrow right after lunch. If you come to the tryouts you'll see."

Jessica looked at Elizabeth. Her eyes sparkled with excitement. "I'm going to get the lead part," she said confidently.

"How do you know?" Elizabeth teased. "Maybe you'll be picked to be the Thanksgiving turkey."

"Very funny," Jessica said. "Just you wait," she added. "I'm going to have a better part than that Mr. Show-off."

# CHAPTER 3

# Time to Audition

On Tuesday, Jessica thought only about the tryouts for the play. Every time she closed her eyes, she daydreamed about being the star.

As soon as lunch was over, she called to Elizabeth and her other friends to hurry up. She and Elizabeth, Lila, Amy, Ellen, and Eva raced down the hallway to the auditorium.

When they reached the auditorium, there was already a big group of kids gathered.

"You just watch," said a familiar voice.

"I'm going to be the star of the show." It was Winston. He was bragging to a group of third graders.

Jessica gave him an angry look. "You are not going to be the star," she grumbled. "Being the star is important and serious. You are just too silly, Winston Egbert."

"Attention! Attention, everybody!" Miss Johnson, one of the third-grade teachers, was speaking into a microphone. Her voice boomed through the auditorium. "Will everyone please take a seat so we can get started."

Jessica pulled Elizabeth to a seat in the front row. She didn't want to miss a word Miss Johnson was saying.

"There are many parts in this play," Miss Johnson said. "And we need second- and third-grade volunteers to help build scenery and to help backstage during the play. If

16

that's what you'd like to do, go to the rear of the auditorium. Mr. Grasso, one of our art teachers, will tell you what to do."

Elizabeth leaned over to Jessica. "I'm going to help with the scenery," she whispered.

"But Liz!" Jessica whispered. "You'll watch me try out, won't you?"

Elizabeth nodded and then walked to the back of the auditorium. Jessica held her breath, waiting for the auditions to begin.

"Let's get started right away," Miss Johnson said. "I'll call classes, and then you can each take turns doing a short performance for us. Say your name before you start."

One by one, the first-grade classes were called. Each student stepped to the front of the stage and said his or her name. Some sang songs or recited short poems they had memorized. Jessica was too impatient to pay any attention. Finally, Miss Johnson spoke into the microphone. "It's time for the second grade. We'll start with Mrs. Otis's class. Line up, please!"

There was a noisy scramble as those in Mrs. Otis's class who wanted parts lined up on stage. Jessica was the very first in line.

"Jessica Wakefield!" she said as she stepped forward. She held out a cassette tape of the music she needed for her dance. Mrs. Otis smiled and put it in the tape player. Then Jessica did a deep curtsy the way her modern dance teacher had taught her.

When the music started, Jessica moved across the stage. She knew everyone was watching her, and she felt a little bit shy. But it was fun. She was sure Miss Johnson and Mrs. Otis thought her dance was wonderful.

"I know a poem, too," she said when she finished. She recited it without making a mistake.

"That was lovely, Jessica," Miss Johnson said, making a note on her clipboard.

"Yes, it was very nice, Jessica," Mrs. Otis said. "Thank you very much."

Smiling from ear to ear, Jessica walked off the stage. As she passed Winston, she gave him a smile. She could be nice to him now that she knew her audition had gone so well.

Lila recited *The Night Before Christmas* and missed only a few lines. Amy did handstands and cartwheels, and Eva sang a song. Then it was Winston's turn.

"This is going to be dumb," Jessica whispered to Lila. They were sitting in the front row again.

Lila giggled. "I know. I can't wait to see what he does."

"I'm Winston Egbert," Winston said loudly. "I'm going to be head of the Pilgrims." He cleared his throat and looked very serious. "Listen, fellow Pilgrims," he began in a deep voice. "It's going to be a tough winter, but I want all of you to work hard. Together we can get through anything."

"He sounds like a gym teacher," Eva whispered. "He's funny!"

Winston walked back and forth across the stage. "I know we don't have anything to eat. That's OK. I know we don't have warm clothing to wear. That's OK."

A few of the girls and boys in the audience started laughing. Winston was making fun of how unlucky the Pilgrims were! Jessica was sure it would make Miss Johnson and Mrs. Otis angry. It wasn't right to make jokes about something so serious. She looked at Lila and shook her head. With a tryout like that, Winston would never get a part—big or small.

# CHAPTER 4

# Audition Results

Elizabeth and Jessica walked quickly through the hall on Wednesday morning.

"Why are you rushing?" Elizabeth asked. "You're never in a hurry to get to school."

"I want to know what part I got," Jessica said, giving Elizabeth's arm a tug. "Mrs. Otis is going to make an announcement. Hurry!"

They ran into the classroom and stopped at the teacher's desk. Everyone else who had auditioned was crowded around, too.

"Please tell us, Mrs. Otis," Eva begged the teacher.

"All right, I know you're all eager to know," Mrs. Otis said. "First, I'm happy to say that everyone who tried out got a part." She smiled, "Jessica, you're an Indian."

Jessica gasped. "I am? The chief Indian? Really?"

"Well, you're not the lead Indian, Jessica. But you will be the leader of the Indian dance. And you'll welcome the audience to the Thanksgiving play."

"Winston," Mrs. Otis continued. "Congratulations. You'll be the Indian chief."

Elizabeth could see how disappointed her sister was. "I'm sorry," she said. "You're in the Indian dance, though. And you'll be the first one to speak."

"But that will only be a few lines. Then I'll

24

have nothing to say," Jessica grumbled. She pouted and dragged her feet to her desk.

"I got a part," Eva said to Elizabeth proudly. "I'm going to be one of the Pilgrims!"

"And I'm a turkey!" Amy laughed. She strutted around, flapping her arms. "Gobble gobble!"

Elizabeth giggled.

"I get to wear a feather headdress," Winston announced. "I have a lot of lines to learn, and I'll be one of the most important people in the play. The Indians were the ones who saved the Pilgrims' lives, you know."

"I know that," Lila said.

Todd and Ken were going to be Pilgrims, too. "Hey, Win," Todd snickered. "Let's see you do a rain dance."

Winston immediately started hopping

around from one foot to the other, yelling and clapping his hands. "This is a real rain dance," he told them. "I saw a tribe do it on TV once."

"Winston's the expert," Ken said. "He knows everything because he's the Indian chief." He and Todd began to laugh.

"I'm glad you got a part," Elizabeth told Winston. "I'm sure you'll be good."

Winston grinned. "I'll be the best Indian chief ever. Hey, Elizabeth. Would you help me learn my part?"

"Well . . ." Elizabeth bit her lip and glanced back at Jessica. She saw that her sister was slouching in her seat with a big frown on her face. Jessica was in a bad mood because Winston had gotten a big part and she hadn't. Elizabeth didn't want to make Jessica angrier.

"Please?" Winston said. "I want to do a really, really good job."

Elizabeth looked at him. Usually Winston didn't act serious. But she could tell he was serious now. The play was important to him.

"OK," she agreed. "I'll help you learn your part."

"Thanks," he said, smiling happily.

When Elizabeth went to her seat, she tried to cheer up Jessica. "It'll be fun to be in the dance, Jess. And you do get to speak."

Jessica didn't say anything.

"I'll bet you'll get to wear a beautiful costume, too," Elizabeth went on. "Mom will make it for you."

Jessica continued to pout. Elizabeth didn't know how to cheer up her sister.

"What was *he* saying to you?" Jessica

asked suddenly. She was glaring across the room at Winston.

Elizabeth shrugged. "He asked if I would help him learn his part. I said yes."

"You did?" Jessica looked surprised. "Thanks a lot," she said.

Elizabeth sighed. She knew nothing she could say would make Jessica feel any better.

# CHAPTER 5

# Quiet, Please!

The first rehearsal for the play was very noisy. The first graders chased each other around the stage. Jessica and the other Indian dancers were whispering as the gym teacher demonstrated the dance steps. Mr. Grasso was trying to keep the scenery painters from splashing paint everywhere. Mrs. Otis was talking to the Pilgrims, and Miss Johnson kept saying, "Let's take it from the top!"

Jessica didn't know what the top was. But she had another idea.

"Miss Johnson?" she said, stepping up behind the teacher.

Miss Johnson turned around and looked confused for a moment. "I don't want the Indian dance yet," she said.

"But Miss Johnson?" Jessica said, putting on her sweetest smile. "I was wondering if I could do a dance solo. I'm a very good dancer. My dance teacher always says so. Couldn't I have a solo?"

"I'm sorry," Miss Johnson replied. "It's a group dance for all the Indian girls to do together. None of the Indians get a solo."

Jessica frowned and looked across the stage at Winston. He was having fun trying to imitate an Indian war cry.

"What about him?" she asked grumpily.

Miss Johnson smiled. "Winston? Oh, of

31

course he has a solo. He's the Indian chief. He has a lot of lines to learn, too."

Jessica got grumpier and grumpier with each word Miss Johnson said. She turned quickly and stomped off to find her sister.

Elizabeth had a paint brush in one hand. "Hi, Jess," she said. "Mr. Grasso is about to bring the fence in. Then I'm going to paint it brown."

"Hey, Jessica," Winston called out. "What are you doing over there? You're supposed to be with the other Indians learning the dance."

"Don't you boss me around, Mr. Show-off," Jessica called.

"You're just jealous," Winston said with a laugh. He looked at the pages of script in his hand. "I have to learn my lines now. Can you test me to see if I know them later?" he asked Elizabeth.

"Sure," Elizabeth answered.

"He's acting like he's King of Second Grade," Jessica said, after Winston had walked away.

"He's just excited, that's all," Elizabeth said.

"He thinks he's a star and can boss everyone around, you mean," Jessica snapped. She went to join the other dancers. *No matter what Winston says, I won't listen to him,* she said to herself.

"No, not that color!" Mr. Grasso shouted from the other side of the stage. Three boys were painting a flat cardboard house yellow. "Gray! All the houses are gray!"

"Where are the town elders?" Mrs. Otis

called out. "Pilgrim leaders? Where are you?"

"I'll get them," Winston said. "They're supposed to be right here."

Jessica joined the other Indian girls. "He's Mr. Know-it-all," she said.

"Yeah, he thinks he's the director," Crystal Burton said. She was in third grade. None of the older kids wanted to be bossed around by a second grader.

All of the teachers were talking at once, and all of the students were talking to each other. Stagehands were carrying pieces of scenery around and bumping into things, and someone was testing the lights.

"The reds are fine!" Mrs. Otis said when there was nothing but red light on the stage. Then all the lights turned to blue.

Mr. Grasso walked past Jessica and the Indians. "This is supposed to turn into a play?" He shook his head and hurried away.

Jessica giggled. "Rehearsals sure are crazy," she said.

Lila nodded. "And boring. This play is going to be awful. I don't know why I tried out."

"It'll be great," Jessica said. Maybe she didn't have a starring part, but she was excited to be in the play. She couldn't wait for the big night.

# CHAPTER 6

# Squash, Corn, and Rice

The next day, Mrs. Otis walked into the classroom with a large grocery bag.

"What's that?" Ellen asked, running over.

"I brought in a surprise for all of you," the teacher said cheerfully. "Real Pilgrim food."

"Oh, Mrs. Otis!" Caroline waved her hand in the air. "Can I help pass things out?"

Elizabeth looked at Jessica and grinned. Caroline was always trying to be the teacher's pet.

"What kind of food do you think it is?" Jessica whispered.

"I don't know," Elizabeth answered.

Everyone watched while Mrs. Otis took containers out of the bag and set everything out on one of the art tables at the back of the classroom. Caroline and two other volunteers helped arrange paper plates, napkins, and plastic forks.

"All right, kids," Mrs. Otis said. "This is going to be an authentic Pilgrim meal. We have parched corn, salted fish, wild rice, squash, onions—"

"Onions! Yuck!" Lila exclaimed. "I never have to eat onions at home."

"The Indians ate onions all the time," Winston said loudly. "You should eat them because you're an Indian in the play. And since I'm the chief, I say you have to."

Lila made a face. "I don't have to do anything you say, Chief Dumbhead, so there."

"OK. That's enough. Now everyone line up," Mrs. Otis said quickly. "Take a little bit of each food. You just need enough to taste."

Elizabeth stood up. She was eager to see what the Pilgrim food was like. Those ahead of her were slow in helping themselves to the food.

"This looks weird," Todd said. He sniffed the squash on his plate. "Didn't they have turkey with cranberry sauce?"

Mrs. Otis laughed. "No, I'm afraid not. Just try a little bit. You'll all survive."

Elizabeth helped herself to very small servings. She nibbled a little bit of the salted fish. It was dry and chewy. She made a face.

"Is it horrible?" Jessica asked her. She hadn't tasted anything yet, and she looked worried.

Elizabeth swallowed the fish quickly. "It's very salty," she said.

"Is this really corn, Mrs. Otis?" Ken asked. "It looks funny."

"It's good," Winston cut in. He stuffed a forkful of corn into his mouth. "Besides, all the Indians ate it," he mumbled.

"How do you know it's good?" Amy said. "I'll bet you never ate any before in your whole life."

"I know, because that's what I say in the play," Winston shot back. He smiled and looked away. "I say to the Pilgrims, 'We share this corn with you. It is good.'"

"It is bad," Charlie said, copying Winston's voice. Everyone laughed, even Mrs. Otis.

Winston stared at Charlie. "Ha ha ha. You're just angry because you're not in the play."

"I didn't even try out," Charlie reminded him.

"Now, now," Mrs. Otis said. "Enough of that. Let's enjoy the rest of our meal." She took a helping of onions and squash.

Elizabeth tried some of the wild rice on her plate. She felt sorry for Winston. Usually, everyone liked him a lot. It was true that he was being a show-off, but he was still the same old likable Winston inside.

"Wait till we get to rehearsal," Jessica said. "I'll make Winston sorry he's such a bossy know-it-all."

Elizabeth sighed. She couldn't wait for the play to be over with. Then everyone would be friends again.

# CHAPTER 7

# Bossy Winston

O ver the weekend, Mrs. Wakefield made Jessica's costume. She had bought lightweight brown fabric and colorful beads at the fabric store.

"Can you make a long dress, Mom?" Jessica asked, after Mrs. Wakefield laid the material out on the kitchen table.

Mrs. Wakefield looked thoughtful. "That would make it difficult for you to dance. Besides, I don't think Indian girls wore long dresses," she said. "We can look in the encyclopedia and see if there's a picture."

"I'll go get the book," Elizabeth said. She ran to the den and came back carrying a heavy book. "We should look under 'I' for Indians."

Jessica helped find the right page. There were pictures of many different Indian tribes.

"This is what I want," Jessica said, pointing to a dress with a long cape made of feathers.

Mrs. Wakefield looked at the picture. "It's beautiful, but we don't have enough feathers to make you a cape like that." She smiled. "Don't worry. I'll make you the perfect Indian costume."

While the twins watched, their mother cut out two rectangles from the material. Then she sewed them together on the machine, leaving holes for Jessica's head and arms.

"Can I try it on yet?" Jessica begged. She was excited about having an Indian dress. She put it on over her clothes.

Their older brother, Steven, walked into the kitchen. "That looks like a big brown bag," he said, laughing.

"It does not," Jessica said angrily.

Mrs. Wakefield held out some beads. "Don't worry. It will look beautiful once I sew on the beads and the fringe," she said.

Jessica twirled around. She was happy that her mother could sew so well, and she was certain she would have the best costume in the play.

"I get to wear a headband, too," she added. "With a real feather in it."

On Monday, Jessica took her new costume to school. "I still wish I could do a dance solo," she said to her sister, as she hung the Indian dress in the costume closet before rehearsal.

"But you get to introduce the play," Elizabeth reminded her. "That's a very important part."

"I guess so. The play is fun, except for Winston. He's so bossy."

The two girls ran to the auditorium. Now that it was Thanksgiving week, the class was going to spend every day rehearsing. The play was only two days away and there was a lot to do.

When the two girls arrived at the auditorium, they were greeted by a familiar voice. "Hey, Jessica!" Winston shouted. "Why aren't you with the other Indians?"

Jessica turned around and looked at Winston. "Hey, Jessica! Why aren't you with the other Indians?" she repeated, making her voice sound just like Winston's. Winston stared at her in surprise.

Jessica then pushed on the backs of her ears so they stuck out, and she mimicked Winston's bossy voice again. "We share this corn with you. It is good," she said loudly.

Some of the other boys and girls looked at her. Lila giggled. "What are you doing, Jessica?"

"I am head of these people," Jessica went on. She had heard Winston say his lines so often that she knew them by heart. "We welcome you to this land."

"She's pretending to be Winston," Amy said with a laugh.

"Cut it out, Jessica," Winston said. His face was red.

"Cut it out," Jessica repeated. She stomped

her feet and walked over to the Indian girls. "Hey, you girls. You're supposed to be practicing your dance now. I'm the Indian chief, and I want your dance to be perfect."

The girls all laughed at her imitation of Winston.

Winston looked angry. "Jessica!" he shouted. "You're ruining the rehearsal."

Jessica didn't pay any attention to him. She was having fun teasing him. And everyone thought she was being very funny. "I'm the best actor in the whole world," Jessica said. "I'm going to be a Hollywood star and be in movies and have a million dollars."

"Oh, Indian chief!" Lila said. "Can I be your friend? I promise to do everything you tell me to."

Jessica shook her head and pushed her ears out again. "I can't be friends with you.

You don't even have any lines to say in this play."

Everyone laughed harder than before. Winston ran after Jessica. "Cut it out!" he said. "You're not funny."

"What's wrong, Win?" Jessica asked. "Are you mad because people are listening to me instead of you?"

Winston's face was bright red. He turned around and stomped away.

"Uh, oh," Lila said. "He's going to tell on you, Jessica."

Jessica shrugged. "I don't care. Now he knows he can't boss me around anymore. That's what matters."

She smiled. Being the center of attention was fun. And she had gotten back at Winston for being such a show-off.

"You teased him a lot," Elizabeth said to

her. "It was very mean to make fun of his ears."

"He deserved it," Jessica said firmly.

Elizabeth felt bad. "You won't make fun of him anymore, will you?" she asked. "Promise?"

Jessica nodded slowly. "OK." She crossed her heart and snapped her fingers twice, making their secret promise sign. "I won't tease him anymore unless he starts bossing me around again."

# CHAPTER 8

# Break a Leg!

The last rehearsal was held on Wednesday morning. That was the day before Thanksgiving and also the day of the performance. After dinner, all of the Wakefields, including Grandma and Grandpa Wakefield, who were visiting, drove to school.

"We have to go backstage to get ready," Jessica told her family once they had arrived.

Mrs. Wakefield gave her a big kiss. "We'll be waiting for you when the play is over.

Break a leg. That's what you're supposed to say to actors for good luck."

"Remember, there's no reason to be nervous," Mr. Wakefield said with a wink.

"I'm not nervous, Dad. I can't wait for you to hear me introduce the play."

"Come on," Elizabeth said, grabbing Jessica's hand. She was excited, too.

When they got backstage, Jessica quickly changed into her Indian dress and put on her headband. "I hope no one forgets the steps of the dance," she said. She jumped up and down on her toes and clapped her hands. "I can't wait!"

"Neither can I," Elizabeth said. She went to Mr. Grasso for her instructions.

"OK," Mr. Grasso told the stage crew. "I need two volunteers to help me open and shut the curtain."

Elizabeth raised her hand.

"Elizabeth," Mr. Grasso said, pointing to her. "And Mark," he said to a third grader.

Everyone who had a part looked nervous and happy at the same time. All of the Pilgrim women were wearing long dresses with aprons, and scarves covering their heads. The Pilgrim men wore tights and short pants that came only to their knees, plus black coats and tall hats.

Someone in a turkey costume ran up to Elizabeth. "Gobble, gobble," said Amy's voice.

"You look like a real turkey," Elizabeth giggled. "Are you nervous about being on stage?"

Amy shook her head. "No. I mean yes. Oh, I don't know." She ran away again.

The Indian girls were quietly practicing their dance, and Jessica was doing all the steps perfectly. The Indian dance was the very first thing in the play, so it was important.

"Places, everybody!" Mrs. Otis called in a loud whisper. "Everybody in your places! The curtain opens in two minutes."

Elizabeth's stomach had butterflies. She was nervous, and she didn't even have to go on stage. She held onto the rope that opened the curtain and squeezed her eyes shut. She wanted to do the best job of opening the curtain.

"Where's Winston?" Miss Johnson called out suddenly. "Has anyone seen Winston?"

Elizabeth gulped. "Isn't he here?" she asked Mark.

"I don't know," Mark whispered. Then he pointed. "There he is."

Winston was wearing a costume with

feathers and beads. He looked like a real Indian chief!

"Let's look at the audience," Mark whispered. He peeked behind the curtain. "You can see everything."

Elizabeth saw that the whole auditorium was filled. Students who weren't in the play were in the audience, too. Parents were dressed up, and everyone was talking cheerfully. Elizabeth could see her mother and father, as well as her grandparents and Steven, in the third row.

"Bring down the houselights," Miss Johnson told the light operators.

While Elizabeth was still peeking, the lights in the auditorium started to grow dim, and everyone stopped talking.

"Quiet on stage!" Mrs. Otis whispered. "Indian girls, take your places."

Jessica and Lila and the other dancers passed by Elizabeth. "Break a leg," Elizabeth whispered to her sister.

"Open the curtain!" Miss Johnson called.

Quickly, Elizabeth, Mark, and Mr. Grasso started pulling on the rope, and the curtains opened in the middle. The audience applauded. Elizabeth couldn't stop smiling.

The audience hushed when Jessica walked to the edge of the stage. Her costume looked beautiful in the bright lights. Elizabeth felt very proud of her sister.

"Welcome to our Thanksgiving play," Jessica said in a loud, clear voice. "The scene is Massachusetts in the year 1621. Members of the Plymouth Colony have survived their first harsh winter in the new world. Join us as they celebrate their first Thanksgiving."

Jessica gave a small curtsy and went back

to the other Indian girls. The music for the dance started. They began their steps. All the girls had bells strapped around their ankles, which made a jingling sound as they danced.

Elizabeth watched with excitement. Everything was so beautiful. She turned around just in time to see Winston. He was supposed to walk onto the stage right after the Indian dance was over.

"Break a leg," she whispered.

Winston took a deep breath, but didn't say anything. Elizabeth had never seen him look so serious.

When the dance was finished, the audience started applauding again. But the Indian girls didn't bow. Miss Johnson had told them that real actors bowed only after the whole play was over.

"OK, Win," Mrs. Otis whispered. "You're on."

Elizabeth held her breath. Winston was finally going to do his part! She knew he had worked very hard, and she was happy for him.

Winston straightened his feather headdress and walked out onto the stage where the lights were blazing bright. He looked out at the audience and opened his mouth to speak his first line, but not a single word came out.

Winston had stage fright!

# CHAPTER 9

# Two Stars of the Show

Jessica could tell something was wrong. Winston had come in at the right time, but he wasn't saying his lines. She turned to look at him. Winston was staring at the audience as though it were a giant monster about to eat him up. Jessica knew he was too scared to do his part.

She wanted to laugh at him. After showing off so much, Winston now looked silly. But Jessica also felt sad for Winston. He must be very embarrassed. If he didn't say his lines, the play would be ruined! His first line was supposed to be "I bring you greetings from my people."

"Greetings, oh chief," Jessica said in a loud voice.

Winston blinked and looked at her. He nodded. "Greetings," he whispered.

Jessica was thinking fast. Winston's next lines were supposed to be "This is the dance of the harvest. We dance to give thanks." But Winston still didn't say anything.

"This is the dance of the harvest," Jessica said, staring right into his eyes. The other Indian girls were looking at each other in surprise.

"We dance to give thanks," Winston said in a hoarse voice.

Jessica nodded a little bit. She wanted to tell him not to be nervous. "What should we do now, chief?" she asked him.

"Umm . . ." Winston looked at the audience again and then quickly looked at Jessica and gulped. "Gather food for the strangers who have come to our land," he said. "For they are starving and—and—"

Jessica wanted to let out a sigh of relief. That was the right line! But she couldn't stop helping him now. "And very sick," she finished for him.

Winston nodded. He turned to the side of the stage where the other Indians would enter. "Come, my people!"

Other Indians began to file onto the stage, and Winston looked relieved. Jessica took a deep breath and looked over to the side. She could just see her sister standing behind the curtain.

Elizabeth waved to her and gave her a very big grin. Jessica had saved the play!

From then on, the performance went exactly as it was supposed to. The Pilgrims told the Indians why they had come to America and asked for their help. The Indians showed them how to plant corn and hunt in the forest.

The last scene had all of the Indians and all of the Pilgrims gathered together to share the Thanksgiving feast. Winston was saying everything correctly, and he was doing a very good job.

"From this day on, we promise to be your friends," he said to the Pilgrims. "Let us give thanks every year for the good things this land gives to us."

Then, everybody turned to face the audience and gave a bow. The parents and teachers and brothers and sisters and other students all started clapping loudly and cheering.

Jessica couldn't stop smiling. Thanks to her, Winston had gotten over his stage fright. When it was time for all of the Indians to take a bow together, Winston looked right at her and smiled.

After the applause had finished, the families of all the actors came up on stage. Every single person wore a proud smile. Mrs. Otis and Miss Johnson looked happiest of all.

"Jessica!" Mrs. Otis said. She gave Jessica a big hug and looked at Mr. and Mrs. Wakefield. "Do you realize Jessica saved the show? Winston was having a little trouble, so Jessica jumped right in and helped him out."

"We're so proud of you, Jessica," Mr. Wakefield said. He gave her a big kiss and hug.

"Oh, Daddy," Jessica said, grinning.

Grandma and Grandpa Wakefield kissed

her, too. "We didn't know what a professional performance we were going to see," Grandpa said. "It was absolutely first-rate."

Jessica looked over at Elizabeth. She knew they were both thinking the same thing: There was more than one way to be the star of the show!

# CHAPTER 10

# Thanksgiving Day

When Elizabeth woke up the next morning, she started thinking about what to wear to school. Then she remembered: There was no school. It was Thanksgiving Day.

"Hey, Jessica!" She reached over and pulled Jessica's blanket back. "Wake up."

"What did you do that for?" Jessica grumbled sleepily. She sat up and stretched.

"It's Thanksgiving!" Elizabeth said. She sat on her knees and grinned. "We get turkey and cranberries and apple pie and pumpkin pie and stuffing and peas and carrots—"

"And stinky salted fish and crummy parched corn," Jessica giggled. "Boy, I'm sure glad we don't have to eat that stuff anymore."

Elizabeth laughed. It was an exciting holiday. She was especially glad to spend the holiday with their grandparents. She and Jessica would get to wear their best dresses.

All morning, everyone helped prepare for the meal. First Jessica and Elizabeth set the table carefully, using their mother's best china and silverware. Then Mr. Wakefield and Grandpa made the turkey stuffing, and Grandma made the pies. Steven helped out, too. He tried all the food.

"To see if it's OK," he explained as he licked pumpkin pie filling off of his finger.

Finally it was time for Thanksgiving dinner. Mrs. Wakefield lit candles on the table, while Mr. Wakefield brought in a large platter with the turkey on it. Just smelling it made Elizabeth's mouth water.

"It looks delicious, Alice," Grandma said. "Just perfect."

Mrs. Wakefield smiled happily.

"And now, before we eat," said Mr. Wakefield. "I think we should take turns saying what each of us is thankful for."

Grandma and Grandpa said they were thankful to be spending Thanksgiving with the people they loved. Mrs. Wakefield said she was thankful for her children. Steven said he was thankful for getting in the junior basketball league. And Mr. Wakefield said he was thankful that they were all healthy and happy.

"And what about you girls?" Grandma asked.

Elizabeth looked at Jessica. "I'm thankful that I have a—"

"Twin sister," Jessica finished for her. "Me, too."

Everyone laughed. "Now pass the turkey, Ned," Grandpa said. "I'm getting pretty hungry!"

As Mr. Wakefield started serving turkey and stuffing, the telephone rang.

"Now, who could that be?" Mrs. Wakefield said. She got up and went to the kitchen to answer the phone.

Elizabeth watched as her father piled food

onto her plate. "I hope I can eat all that," she said.

Then she heard her mother's voice. "Oh! How wonderful!" Mrs. Wakefield exclaimed.

Everyone at the table stopped talking to listen.

"Congratulations," Mrs. Wakefield went on. She sounded very happy and excited. "And Thanksgiving is such a wonderful day for it, too. Well, give her our best wishes. And we'll see her when she gets home from the hospital. Bye-bye."

Elizabeth's eyes were round with curiosity. "I wonder who that was," she whispered to Jessica.

"I don't know," Jessica said through a mouthful of stuffing.

Mrs. Wakefield came back into the dining

room. She had a wide smile on her face. "That was Mr. DeVito from next door," she explained. "Mrs. DeVito just had a little baby girl!"

"Wow!" Jessica gasped. "A baby girl!"

"And he said we're all invited to come see her as soon as they bring her home from the hospital."

Elizabeth grinned. It was great news! "Does she have a name? What does she look like?"

"They should call her Ashley Kendra Suzette," Jessica announced. "Those are my favorite names."

"They're calling her Jenny," Mrs. Wakefield said. "And you'll get to see her next week."

Elizabeth took a large bite of turkey.

"Won't it be fun having a baby girl living next door?" she asked.

"Yes!" Jessica said. "It's almost as much fun as having a baby sister of our own."

*Will Jessica and Elizabeth decide they want a baby sister of their own? Find out in Sweet Valley Kids #14, JESSICA THE BABY-SITTER.*

# COULD *YOU* BE THE NEXT SWEET VALLEY READER OF THE MONTH?

## ENTER BANTAM BOOKS' SWEET VALLEY CONTEST & SWEEPSTAKES IN ONE!

### Calling all Sweet Valley Fans! Here's a chance to appear in a Sweet Valley book!

We know how important Sweet Valley is to you. That's why we've come up with a Sweet Valley celebration offering exciting opportunities to have YOUR thoughts printed in a Sweet Valley book!

### "How do I become a Sweet Valley Reader of the Month?"

It's easy. Just write a one-page essay (no more than 150 words, please) telling us a little about yourself, and why you like to read Sweet Valley books. We will pick the best essays and print them along with the winner's photo in the back of upcoming Sweet Valley books. Every month there will be a new Sweet Valley Kids Reader of the Month!

### And, there's more!

Just sending in your essay makes you eligible for the Grand Prize drawing for a trip to Los Angeles, California! This once-in-a-life-time trip includes round-trip airfare, accommodations for 5 nights (economy double occupancy), a rental car, and meal allowance. (Approximate retail value: $4,500.)

Don't wait! Write your essay today.
No purchase necessary. See the next page for Official rules.

# ENTER BANTAM BOOKS' SWEET VALLEY READER OF THE MONTH SWEEPSTAKES

**OFFICIAL RULES:**

### READER OF THE MONTH ESSAY CONTEST

1. <u>No Purchase Is Necessary.</u> Enter by hand printing your name, address, date of birth and telephone number on a plain 3" x 5" card, and sending this card along with your essay telling us about yourself and why you like to read Sweet Valley books to:

**READER OF THE MONTH
SWEET VALLEY KIDS
BANTAM BOOKS
YR MARKETING
666 FIFTH AVENUE
NEW YORK, NEW YORK 10103**

2. <u>Reader of the Month Contest Winner.</u> For each month from June 1, 1990 through December 31, 1990, a Sweet Valley Kids Reader of the Month will be chosen from the entries received during that month. The winners will have their essay and photo published in the back of an upcoming Sweet Valley Kids title.

3. Enter as often as you wish, but each essay must be original and each entry must be mailed in a separate envelope bearing sufficient postage. All completed entries must be postmarked and received by Bantam no later than December 31, 1990, in order to be eligible for the Essay Contest and Sweepstakes. Entrants must be between the ages of 6 and 16 years old. Each essay must be no more than 150 words and must be typed double-spaced or neatly printed on one side of an 8 1/2" x 11" page which has the entrant's name, address, date of birth and telephone number at the top. The essays submitted will be judged each month by Bantam's Marketing Department on the basis of originality, creativity, thoughtfulness, and writing ability, and all of Bantam's decisions are final and binding. Essays become the property of Bantam Books and none will be returned. Bantam reserves the right to edit the winning essays for length and readability. Essay Contest winners will be notified by mail within 30 days of being chosen. In the event there are an insufficient number of essays received in any month which meet the minimum standards established by the judges, Bantam reserves the right not to choose a Reader of the Month. Winners have 30 days from the date of Bantam's notice in which to respond, or an alternate Reader of the Month winner will be chosen. Bantam is not responsible for incomplete or lost or misdirected entries.

4. Winners of the Essay Contest and their parents or legal guardians may be required to execute an Affidavit of Eligibility and Promotional Release supplied by Bantam. Entering the Reader of the Month Contest constitutes permission for use of the winner's name, address, likeness and contest submission for publicity and promotional purposes, with no additional compensation.

5. Employees of Bantam Books, Bantam Doubleday Dell Publishing Group, Inc., and their subsidiaries and affiliates, and their immediate family members are not eligible to enter the Essay Contest. The Essay Contest is open to residents of the U.S. and Canada (excluding the province of Quebec), and is void wherever prohibited or restricted by law. All applicable federal, state, and local regulations apply.

### READER OF THE MONTH SWEEPSTAKES

6. Sweepstakes Entry. No purchase is necessary. Every entrant in the Sweet Valley High, Sweet Valley Twins and Sweet Valley Kids Essay Contest whose completed entry is received by December 31, 1990 will be entered in the Reader of the Month Sweepstakes. The Grand Prize winner will be selected in a random drawing from all completed entries received on or about February 1, 1991 and will be notified by mail. Bantam's decision is final and binding. Odds of winning are dependent on the number of entries received. The prize is non-transferable and no substitution is allowed. The Grand Prize winner must be accompanied on the trip by a parent or legal guardian. Taxes are the sole responsibility of the prize winner. Trip must be taken within one year of notification and is subject to availability. Travel arrangements will be made for the winner and, once made, no changes will be allowed.

7. 1 Grand Prize. A six day, five night trip for two to Los Angeles, California. Includes round-trip coach airfare, accommodations for 5 nights (economy double occupancy), a rental car — economy model, and spending allowance for meals. (Approximate retail value: $4,500.)

8. The Grand Prize winner and their parent or legal guardian may be required to execute an Affidavit of Eligibility and Promotional Release supplied by Bantam. Entering the Reader of the Month Sweepstakes constitutes permission for use of the winner's name, address, and the likeness for publicity and promotional purposes, with no additional compensation.

9. Employees of Bantam Books, Bantam Doubleday Dell Publishing Group, Inc., and their subsidiaries and affiliates, and their immediate family members are not eligible to enter this Sweepstakes. The Sweepstakes is open to residents of the U.S. and Canada (excluding the province of Quebec), and is void wherever prohibited or restricted by law. If a Canadian resident, the Grand Prize winner will be required to correctly answer an arithmetical skill-testing question in order to receive the prize. All applicable federal, state, and local regulations apply. The Grand Prize will be awarded in the name of the minor's parent or guardian. Taxes, if any, are the winner's sole responsibility.

10. For the name of the Grand Prize winner and the names of the winners of the Sweet Valley High, Sweet Valley Twins and Sweet Valley Kids Essay Contests, send a stamped, self-addressed envelope entirely separate from your entry to: Bantam Books, Sweet Valley Reader of the Month Winners, Young Readers Marketing, 666 Fifth Avenue, New York, New York 10103. The winners list will be available after April 15, 1991.